MAMA CAT

Marcie S. Jones

Illustrated by Henry J. Kouche

Mama Cat
by
Marcie S. Jones

© 2003

Illustrations by Henry J. Kouche

Author Photo on page 65 by Ashley Burke

Design by Amy G. Moore

Library of Congress Catalog Card Number: 2003110376
ISBN: 1890306495

Warwick House Publishing
720 Court Street
Lynchburg, VA 24504

*To my husband and children
with all my love*

CONTENTS

CHAPTER 1
The Weary Traveler

Mama Cat paused in her journey. The day had been another hot, humid one in Virginia. The summer was full of days like these in the central area of the state. Sometimes the only way Mama Cat could separate one day from another was because night came between the long days.

The large oak tree on the other side of the dry field looked inviting. Its green branches promised a respite from the mid-afternoon heat. As she looked beseechingly at the tree and its cool invitation, she scanned the area for other animals, both two- and four-legged.

Two-legged creatures were sometimes more dangerous than those with four legs. At least with a four-legged animal, Mama Cat stood a chance of outwitting or outrunning it. A human often times was not so easy to evade. Humans had weapons that could hurt stray animals.

Stray animal. How had she become one of those?

Mama Cat looked back at her life. She was only three years old and already she was an outcast. Her original family did not want her anymore. The man had dropped her off at the dump when he found she was pregnant.

A few days at that place had shown her that it was not where she wanted to be. Wild animals came out at night scavenging for food. Mama Cat did not have the energy to deal with those creatures. She had pulled herself together and begun her trek towards a new and hopefully better life.

After several days of walking through fields during the day and hiding in trees at night, Mama Cat knew she had to find a place of her own. Her babies would be coming soon and she wanted a safe home for them.

That's when the sprawling oak tree had come into her vision.

As she walked carefully towards it, she eyed the old farmhouse it shaded. The house seemed quiet, but that could mean the owners were gone. She had learned at her first house that humans did not stay at home all the time. They came and they went as they chose to.

Mama Cat wasn't sure if she wanted a family to live in the white farmhouse or not. While a family might adopt her, it might also chase her off. If the house proved to be uninhabited, she might have a wonderful home for her kittens.

Just as she lay down under the cool tree branches and closed her eyes, she heard a human voice, a little girl's voice. A dog's yapping quickly followed. Oh, no, she thought, I've got to get out of here fast.

Before Mama Cat could pick up her unwieldy body, a redheaded child came running around the far corner of the house with a small dog trotting at her heels. The girl came to an abrupt halt when she spotted Mama Cat. The dog saw Mama Cat at the same time and immediately started growling.

Mama Cat stood, her fur on end, her eyes bright with fear.

"Hush, Maggy," said the girl. "It's just a cat. You know what they are, like Miss Kitty in the house."

The girl's admonition did nothing to stop Maggy and her growling.

Just then the front door to the house creaked open. A woman who looked like an older version of the little girl stepped onto the porch.

"Bridget Noelle, what are you doing out here in the middle of this hot day when you're supposed to be in your room resting for the party tonight?"

"Shh, Mommy. I'm sorry, Maggy needed to go out and I took her and when we got ready to come in we saw that cat. Look, isn't she beautiful?" The words came tumbling out of the child's mouth.

Mrs. Brown shook her head at her daughter. That child could wrap just about anyone around her fingers. Then she looked to where her daughter was pointing. Wonderful, she thought, just what we need, another stray cat and a pregnant one at that.

"Now, Bridget," Mrs. Brown began. "You know we can't keep every animal that shows up at our house. We already have cows and pigs and goats and rabbits and dogs and cats. This one will just have to move on."

3

"But Mommy, she's going to have babies. And she's hot and she's tired. And besides she's a calico cat and you know Aunt Janis says calico cats are magical. We have to keep her."

"Bridget, we don't know where this cat came from. She could have rabies for all we know. Look at the way she's eyeing us right now."

"Please, Mommy, can't we just give her some water and maybe some of Miss Kitty's food? She's just hot and tired and hungry. That's why she looks like she does."

"You know what your daddy says about feeding strays, honey. It just entices them to stay."

"Please, Mommy. Suppose she's the blessed mother of the cat world? We could be turning away the baby Jesus of the animals."

How do you fight the logic of a child like that? wondered Mrs. Brown, as she gave an exasperated sigh.

"All right, Bridget, a small bowl of water and a small bowl of food. But let me do it. I do not want you near that cat. Do you understand me?"

Bridget's small face lit up with a smile. She used her best "yes ma'am" as she scooted up the porch steps to hug her mother.

Mama Cat had watched this entire scene with apprehension. She stayed in her place under the tree, ready to bolt if Maggy took one step near her. She could deal with Maggy; it was the humans who had her worried.

The discussion had mesmerized her. She could follow human talk fairly well. She knew the little girl wanted her to stay and that Mrs. Brown was not pleased with the idea. She also knew by the sparkle in Bridget's eyes that she loved animals, and she could sweet talk her mother into seeing things her way.

As the woman and child retreated into the dark interior of the house, Mama Cat realized that the old oak tree just might offer her the solace she was searching for. She would eat and drink what she was given. She would rest awhile and look the place over. Then she would make her decision as to whether or not she would stay.

Rabies, huh, she thought, as she lay down. What kind of cat do they think I am?

CHAPTER 2
Calico Charm

Mama Cat awoke with a start at the slam of a car door. She silently watched as two boys walked towards the white house. She didn't think either one paid any attention to her as they dragged their baseball bats and gloves in the gravel behind them and groaned about playing baseball in the sweltering heat.

She discovered she was wrong as they climbed the porch stairs.

"Did you see that cat in front of the oak tree, Michael?" asked the smaller of the two. "She sure is pretty. A calico. Aunt Janis would love her."

"I know," replied Michael. "Too bad she found her way to Virginia instead of Georgia. I bet Bridget's trying to talk Mom into letting her keep her. I wonder who's winning the battle, Hunter."

"I wonder what Dad's going to say when he gets home," pondered Hunter. "He doesn't mind a couple of extra outdoor cats, but this one looks pregnant. And we don't know anything about her."

"She must've belonged to someone. She didn't run when we walked by her. That usually means the animal has been around humans."

"Do you think someone is looking for her, Michael?"

"I don't know. I know she doesn't belong to any of the neighbors. We know what their cats look like. Let's get something to drink and find out the story. It oughta be good."

At the mention of drinking, Mama Cat approached the water bowl Mrs. Brown had brought out to her earlier. The water had turned warm since she had first lapped it. It still tasted good though. It was probably one of the reasons the boys had caught her napping. Her thirst had been quenched and her stomach filled for the first time in days. Exhaustion had taken over and she had drifted off to sleep. She'd have to be careful not to do that too much. You never knew where

7

danger hid. She was lucky this time. The boys were curious about her, but they had learned through the years never to approach an unknown animal, even one in their own front yard.

As she lay back down, Mama Cat listened as the family discussed her. The boys and their mother sat in rocking chairs on the front porch while Bridget sat in her mother's lap. Maggy hovered close to Bridget with the stance of a guard dog, albeit a small one. Mama Cat knew not to antagonize dogs, especially the wee ones. The little dogs, for instance rat terriers like Maggy, just didn't know they were little and attacked with ferocity when challenged. Mama Cat would take a big dog any day of the week. She could outrun them.

"The cat's pretty, Mom," said Hunter, as he blew his straight, red hair out of his eyes. "What do you think Dad's going to say about her?"

"I don't know, honey. The cat has only been here a few hours. She doesn't look dangerous. Just hot, tired, and very pregnant. Your dad may not have any objections. On the other hand, we don't know where she came from or where she's been."

"We know she's not local," commented Michael, as he tried to push a stray brown curl off his forehead. "We know all the local animals. Maybe Kevin and Doug know who she belongs to. Maybe she came from their end of the road."

"Maybe. Why don't you give them a call and ask?"

Just then Bridget piped in. "Don't be giving my cat away. She just found us. She needs us. Look at her. She's beautiful with her brown and black spots. And I bet Daddy will let her stay. He needs a good mouser for the barn. I know she's a good mouser. I can tell by the way she looks at me."

"Yeah, right, Bridget. When did you become such an authority on mousers? Anyway, you can't tell a cat is a mouser by the way she looks at you. You have to see her catch mice." Hunter and Michael exchanged knowing looks as Hunter passed this piece of information along to his sister.

"I can too tell by looking at her. I have Celtic blood in me. It helps me see things other people don't see."

"You and your Celtic blood. Michael and I have the same blood and the same relatives as you. Why can't we see these things?"

"You just don't look hard enough, Hunter. Also I'm a girl and we do these things better than boys, right Mommy?"

"Oh no you don't. I'm not getting in the middle of this one. However, I will say that some people can see things that others can't. You all come from wonderful Celtic ancestors. I suspect that if you and your brothers put your minds to it, you would find some of that magic that your grandma talks about. In the meantime, let's get inside and start getting dinner ready. Your father will be home soon. If we have dinner on the table, maybe we'll have time for a swim before bedtime."

Mama Cat just stared as the family walked into the house. What different humans she thought. Bridget could tell she was a good mouser just by looking at her. She hadn't convinced her brothers of that fact, but that was something Mama Cat could help her with. All of these sheds near the house must shelter mice. That could be her ticket in. Maybe she could stay here. She'd have to think about this. A new home sounded so good to her. A home for her babies. Yes, she'd definitely have to think about this.

CHAPTER 3
Decision Time

The pool water felt wonderful at the end of the hot day. One of the favorite pool games for Michael, Hunter, and Bridget was wave making. They did this by jumping up and down in unison until the water formed waves that splashed over the side. They would have made waves until bedtime had their mother not

told them they were making her seasick, which was their goal of course. With groans of "Oh Mom, c'mon," the three stopped jumping and began swimming races.

Mama Cat watched their water play with interest. She'd seen pools before; that's one reason she kept her distance. One of the boys at her former house had wanted to see if cats could swim. Before she knew what was happening, she found herself gasping for air and clawing at the side of the pool. The boy had gotten what was coming to him when his mother saw what he had done. For two weeks he could only watch as others swam and he had to turn over his allowance to help pay for repairs to the vinyl siding of the pool that Mama Cat had destroyed in her panic. Mama Cat had learned her lesson too—keep a safe distance from swimming pools.

Despite the lesson she had learned, Mama Cat crept closer to the pool in hopes of learning what Mr. Brown had to say about her presence. Hearing was made more difficult because Maggy yapped every time Bridget got out of the pool for another jump.

Mama Cat's perseverance was rewarded when she heard Michael ask what his father thought about the stray cat.

"I'm not sure," his dad replied. "I only caught a glimpse of her as I walked in the door. She looked worn out, which is not surprising considering she's a stray. I just hope y'all haven't fed her. That will only make her want to stay. She's probably looking for a place to have those babies and anyone offering her comfort will find themselves with several kittens on their hands."

Mrs. Brown and the children looked at each other when they heard dad's comments. Uh oh, they thought. Their Celtic telepathy was working just fine.

"Well, Boo, I hate to tell you this but I did feed and water the poor thing. She looked so hot and tired; I just had to do something for her. I know what it's like to be pregnant during the summer."

"Mariah, you know how I feel about strays. We've had about a dozen different cats since we moved into this house. I don't mind two or three outdoor cats, but a pregnant cat means we'll have to find homes for the kittens. You know how picky these three are about the homes they'll let their kittens go to. We almost never gave away the kittens from Jezebel's last litter."

"You're right. But I just couldn't chase this cat away."

"Daddy," pleaded Bridget, twirling a wet, red curl in her finger as she looked up at him with big, green eyes. "Please, this is a calico cat. She's magical. We have to keep her. Remember the story of Mary and the baby Jesus? We can't turn out Mama Cat!"

"Mama Cat, is it? You've already named her?"

"Yes sir. She is a mama cat and she looks so lonely. And she'll catch mice, I just know it."

"Dad, we do need another mouser. Remember the litter of mice we found across the road earlier this summer? A good cat could help with those," said Hunter.

13

How could anyone forget the litter of baby mice the children had brought home several weeks ago? They were so thrilled with the tiny creatures that they carried them home in their hands. Their mother still gave a shiver as she recalled seeing so many rodents at one time. And in the hands of her own children. She informed them immediately that those mice were to be returned to their nest. Under no circumstances would they be allowed on the Brown's farm. One look at their mother's face had convinced the children that protesting would do them no good. They turned and slowly made their way back across to the babies' nest.

"You've got a point there about needing a good mouser, Hunter, but what about rabies? You know cases have been reported in this area."

"Can't we just feed and water her, Dad? If she has rabies, she'll start acting weird soon. Can't we just keep our distance for a while?" asked Michael.

"Okay, here's what we'll do. We'll put food and water under the oak tree for the cat, but we won't try to approach her. Understood?"

"Yes sir," three voices chimed in unison.

"When she has those kittens, we won't try to find where she hides them until we know for sure she's okay. That's the deal."

"Thanks, Daddy," smiled Bridget. "Wait until I tell Aunt Janis that we have a magical cat like her Una. Maybe they're related. Oh, and wait until our cousins come for the fourth of July! We'll have kittens to show them."

"Bridget, remember what I told you. We are not going to look for kittens until we know the cat is well."

"I know, Daddy, but still I can dream."

Mama Cat sighed in relief. She agreed with Bridget. She could still dream.

CHAPTER 4
The Mouser at Work

Mama Cat waited patiently behind the old oak tree. She was starting to think of the tree as hers since she had spent so much time around it during the past twenty-four hours.

As she nervously peered around the tree again, she heard the squeak of the front door as it opened in the early morning sunshine. Mama Cat could hardly wait

for the Brown family to see her present for them. She had spent part of the previous night searching for exactly the right thing. She hoped they would appreciate her gesture.

Mr. Brown stepped out the door and came to an abrupt halt. "Honey, come on out here and see what our new cat has left us."

Mrs. Brown came to the door to see what her husband was talking about. "Uh oh," she said. "I wonder if Bridget will understand the meaning of this."

Both Mr. and Mrs. Brown looked at the small, dead mouse lying on their porch. They both knew that this was a gift from Mama Cat, as it is the nature of cats to bring rodents home to their families as a symbol of appreciation. They knew the boys understood this. They also knew that despite Bridget's boasting of Mama Cat being a good mouser, she truly didn't understand all that went with the job.

As Mr. Brown looked into the yard, he saw Mama Cat watching them. "Mama Cat is behind the oak tree. I bet she's waiting for us to give her some praise."

"As much as I don't like mice in my house, I'll be happy to tell her how wonderful she is," replied Mrs. Brown. "I still have visions of chasing a mouse around the kitchen with a broom. The kids loved it. There I was jumping from chair to chair, swinging the broom and hollering at that mouse to get out of my home. It's a wonder it didn't drop dead from fright. The last I saw of that rodent was its long, gray tail as Michael held open the back door for its escape route. It still gives me shivers!"

Just then, a sleepy Bridget appeared at the front door. "Daddy, you didn't kiss me goodbye," she yawned, as she rubbed the sleep from her eyes.

"I wasn't quite ready to leave yet, punkin. I was just stepping outside to check on the cows before leaving for work," commented Mr. Brown, as he tried to hide the dead mouse from Bridget.

"Why are you standing so funny, Daddy?"

"I'm trying to get as much sunshine as I can before I have to stay in the office all day."

"Why are you on the porch, Mommy? You don't check the cows in the morning. And it's not time to feed the chickens."

Mr. and Mrs. Brown looked at each other and then at Bridget.

"Bridget, do you remember telling us last night that Mama Cat was a good mouser?" asked Mrs. Brown.

"Yes, ma'am."

"Well, in the animal world, animals like to give presents to their people and to each other. But their gifts aren't like the ones that we give each other. They can't buy things, so they give things they find in nature."

"Kind of like when I pick flowers for you?" Bridget questioned.

"Kind of," said Mrs. Brown, "only animals choose other types of presents. For instance, a dog might bring a lost slipper to you. A cat might bring something she's found, like a dead mouse. Cats sometimes bring moles or other rodents to the homes of their people. These are their gifts to us."

"Wow," said Bridget, her eyes growing big. "Do you think Mama Cat will do that for us since we're going to adopt her?"

Relief poured through Bridget's parents.

"I think Mama Cat already has," said Mr. Brown.

He picked up his daughter and showed her the mouse. He pointed to Mama Cat who was still watching them.

"She's waiting for us to tell her thank you and then when we leave, she'll take the mouse away," he explained.

"Thanks, Mama Cat. You can stay," yelled Bridget. "Hurry, y'all, let's go back inside so Mama Cat can get the mouse," she urged her parents.

"I'm amazed," said Mrs. Brown to her husband, as they followed their daughter inside. "Why is it that children accept the way nature works better than many adults?"

"It's part of being a child growing up in the country, dear," replied her husband.

Mama Cat smiled to herself as the family closed the front door. She was adopted! Her night's work had brought her a home and people who understood her.

Now she could put her energy into finding a good place on the farm to have her babies.

CHAPTER 5
It's Alive!

Mama Cat watched as Michael and Hunter and their friends hiked down the hill towards the creek. She had heard them tell their mother earlier that they were going exploring in the woods with Kevin, Doug, and Christian. Even though Hunter and Christian were younger than Michael, Kevin, and Doug, the older boys occasionally let them join their expeditions. This was one of those times.

Ladened with backpacks filled with food, water, and other necessities of explorers, the boys began their journey.

Mama Cat decided to tag along, at a distance of course. This might be a perfect time to learn about the farm. What better guides than boys who had spent years finding out what was inside every building and behind every hill?

As they descended, the boys held the branches of the pine trees for the person following. They called out things like "loose rocks ahead" and "cow pile" so that all would know what dangers lurked ahead. Mama Cat was happy for the warnings. They made her walk easier.

A winding creek flowed at the end of the trail. Next to it stood an old tobacco barn.

Hmm, thought Mama Cat, I wonder what it looks like inside?

Obviously Hunter and Christian wanted to know too, since they lifted the wooden latch that was keeping the door closed.

"Be careful of snakes," warned Michael, as the younger boys disappeared into the building.

"We're making too much noise for snakes, Michael," responded Hunter. "Remember that Dad always said if we make enough noise, we'll scare the snakes away."

"Be careful anyway."

A couple of minutes later, the curious duo stepped back into the light. They brushed spider webs from their hair as they made their report to the older guys.

"It still smells like tobacco and it's still full of bugs and spiders. When does that smell ever leave?" asked Christian.

"I don't know," said Kevin. "I know they haven't hung tobacco in it for at least twenty years. You'd think the smoky smell would go away."

"Don't you remember going to Monticello?" asked Michael. "When we went to the kitchen area beneath the house, we went into the smoke house. It still smelled like bacon. And it's been a long time since Thomas Jefferson and his family lived there!"

"Do you think people will come to this tobacco barn in a hundred years and still smell the tobacco?" asked Christian.

"I don't think this tobacco barn will last another hundred years for anyone to come visit it," replied Doug. "And anyway, why would anyone want to see this dirty old tobacco barn?"

Good point, thought Mama Cat, as she listened to the conversation from behind one of the pine trees. I certainly don't want to have my kittens in that barn! Spiders! Not near my babies.

"Come on, y'all, let's get going. I've had enough of old smoke and spider webs. Why don't we walk up the creek and go for a swim near the big flat rock?"

No sooner had Michael said the words than they all took off towards their favorite swimming area in the creek.

As the group approached the rock, they noticed something long and black on it.

"It's a snake," yelled Michael. "Run!"

Yelling and screaming erupted as the boys scattered in different directions. Two ran up the hill into the woods, one jumped into the creek, and another one headed back towards the tobacco barn.

"Wait a minute," called Hunter, as he gingerly approached the rock. Ever curious, Hunter wanted to know why a snake would just lie there when the world around him was in chaos.

"He's dead, y'all. Come on back."

The boys laughed at themselves as they approached the rock where the snake lay. They were hoping none of their friends would find out that they ran from a dead snake. Just as they got up the nerve to pick it up with a stick, the snake sprang to life with a hiss!

"It's alive!!"

The group was gone in a flash.

Well, thought Mama Cat, shaking with laughter at the antics of the youths. Life in the country certainly is interesting. I wonder what will happen next?

CHAPTER 6
Chicken Feed

Mama Cat decided it was time to visit the rest of the Brown's farm. After yesterday's adventure with the boys at the creek, she decided she would go wandering by herself this time. The clucking of the chickens drew her to their lot in the backyard.

She watched the chickens carefully as she ventured near the fenced-in yard. She had never been this close to chickens before. She had seen some in her travels, but had always steered clear of them. Mama Cat wasn't sure she even wanted to be this close to them. After all, they made a lot of noise and were forever kicking up dust.

How on earth do their mothers get them clean after a day in the dirt? wondered Mama Cat. She knew the mother hens couldn't lick their chicks like mother cats licked their kittens. So exactly how did chickens bathe?

"Mommy, Lori's water jug is splashing," said Bridget, as she approached the chicken lot door.

"That's okay, honey," replied Mrs. Brown. "It's a hot day. The water probably feels good anyway. We can always get the chickens more water if they need it."

"Then can I spill my water on me?" asked Bridget.

"Suppose we see who can water the chickens without spilling any more water? Then we'll all go for a quick swim."

"Whoopee!" Bridget and Lori hollered their approval of the plan.

Lori was Bridget's closest friend. She, too, had curly hair, only her ringlets were blonde. Lori and her sister Stacy stayed with the Brown family during the day while their parents worked. Occasionally, Lori would spend the night. Life with Bridget and Lori sometimes made Mrs. Brown very happy that she did not have twins.

Mama Cat watched as Bridget, Lori, and Mrs. Brown quickly opened the chicken lot door. They had to be fast so the chickens wouldn't escape and so that Maggy didn't get in the chicken lot. Maggy liked to chase the chickens. And it was hard to catch chickens once they got out of the lot. Chickens might not have large brains, but they could certainly play a great game of chase.

The chickens came running towards the little girls.

"Okay, okay," said Bridget, "I'm going to feed and water you."

"They sure are hungry today," observed Lori.

"We are a little late in feeding them," responded Mrs. Brown. "They like to eat before now, but I got behind in the chores. Let's check for eggs when we finish with this."

Checking for eggs could be scary sometimes. Some of the mother hens didn't want to get off their nests. You had to be quick—reach under the hen, grab the egg, and move before you got pecked.

"One, two, three, four, five, six!"

"We found six eggs today, Mommy!" exclaimed Bridget.

"Six eggs, great!" replied Mrs. Brown.

"That's more than we found yesterday," said Lori. "Do we have enough to make a cake?"

"We certainly do have enough to make a cake. We'll do that tomorrow. Now let's hurry up and finish so we can go for that swim."

At the mention of swimming, Bridget and Lori scampered towards the chicken house door.

Just then one of the hens decided to take a short flight. As she flew over the startled girls' heads, they screamed and dropped to the floor.

Empty water jugs soared in the air. Eggs sailed into the chicken lot, landing with a splat.

The chickens, frightened by the shrieking girls, flapped their wings as they ran in circles.

Maggy started yapping at the top of her lungs.

Oh, my, thought Mama Cat, as she watched the commotion. I guess they won't have that cake after all.

CHAPTER 7
Watch Out Below

Mama Cat yawned and stretched. She was lying in her favorite spot under the big oak tree. She watched as the Brown children and several of their friends hiked through the freshly mown cow pasture to the barn.

The barn was a two-story, weathered structure. Its gray boards had never seen paint, even when new. The front of the barn sat back from the road. The middle of the front didn't have a door. It was used to park farm equipment.

The area on either side served as storage space for hay and corn. The lower part, which was open on the side closest to the house, also held the troughs from which the cows ate in the winter. The entire building was topped with a tin roof.

"Cow pile," yelled Bridget, as she climbed the hill towards the barn.

"Shh!" said Michael. "If you talk too loud the cows will think we're coming to feed them. Then we'll have to run to the barn."

"Well I like feeding the cows," replied Bridget.

"I do too," said Michael, "but not in the middle of the field and especially not without a bucketful of corn."

"Have you seen Miss Piggy lately?" asked Hunter. "I think she's getting ready to have her calf."

"How can you tell?" asked Brandon, one of the Brown's cousins. "Miss Piggy is so fat, she always looks like she's going to have a baby."

Mama Cat could clearly hear the laughter Brandon's statement brought. Goodness, how big is Miss Piggy? she thought. I wonder if they gave her that name because she eats so much or because she is so big?

Mama Cat decided to follow the children to the barn. She had passed it on her way to the house last week. Now she could examine it closely.

"I love the way the hay smells in the barn," exclaimed Bridget, as she took a deep breath of the sweet air.

"Me too," said Lori.

"The hay does smell good," agreed Hunter, "but I could do without the cow manure."

"At least it smells better than the pigs," responded Michael. "Ooee, those pigs stink!"

Wow, thought Mama Cat, if pigs smell worse than this, I certainly don't want to be around them.

"Be careful getting up into the loft," cautioned Michael, as the children ascended the wooden ladder that leaned against the wall. "It's a long way down and Mom would not be happy if one of us took the fast way to the ground."

The next sounds that Mama Cat heard were those of the children laughing as they jumped from hay bale to hay bale.

"How many hay bales do you think are up here?" asked Christopher, Brandon's brother.

"About fifty million," replied Bridget.

"No, Bridget," said Michael. "There are about 500 bales here. Hunter and I counted as we helped Dad stack them."

"Boy, that was one hot day," commented Hunter. "Why is it that we always bale hay on the hottest day of summer and cut firewood on the coldest day of winter?"

"That's exactly what I asked Dad when we were baling hay," said Michael.

"What did he say?" Brandon wanted to know.

"He said we were just lucky."

The children's giggles floated down the ladder.

Mama Cat began exploring the lower level of the barn as the hay bale jumpers continued their activities.

She peered into the feedboxes first. Some still had old hay in them. The feedboxes were where the cows munched their hay during the cold winter months when there wasn't any grass in the pastures.

Next Mama Cat jumped onto the grain bin. She could smell the corn that was stored in it from last summer. The new corn was still on the stalks. It wouldn't be ready for another month or so.

Just then Mama Cat heard a noise.

"Psst, psst."

She looked around to see where it was coming from.

"Here, Mama Cat, I'm up here," whispered Bridget, her red curls falling across her face as she peered over the side of the loft.

At first all Mama Cat saw was Bridget's hair, eyes, and nose.

As Bridget scooted closer to the edge, Mama Cat watched her shoulders and arms appear.

"Come on Mama Cat. You're so pretty. Come play with us. You'll like jumping on the hay bales." Bridget crawled even closer to the edge of the second floor. Now she was beckoning Mama Cat with both her arms.

The little girl was so intent on getting Mama Cat to come to her that she paid no attention to the fact that there was nothing between her and the lower level of the barn except air. Air might work well for birds and planes, but children could not fly.

Mama Cat's motherly instinct told her she needed to do something before Bridget came tumbling from the upper floor.

"Meow. Meoww. Meowww!" Mama Cat started crying in her loudest voice.

"Meoww. Meowww. Meowww!"

"Who's that meowing?" asked Brandon.

As Hunter scanned the bales of hay looking for the mewing cat, he noticed that Bridget was nowhere to be seen.

"Where's Bridget?" he asked the group.

Michael turned his head towards his brother.

"What do you mean 'where's Bridget'? She's supposed to be with you and Christopher."

"Well, she's not. She left us a few minutes ago. I thought she was with you on the other side of the bales."

Lori decided that this was a good time to take her thumb out of her mouth and show the boys where their sister was.

"She's over there," pointed Lori.

The entire group followed Lori's finger.

All they could see was a pair of legs kicking in the air.

Lickety split, Michael ran towards those legs!

"Bridget Noelle Brown, what do you think you are doing hanging over the side of the barn? Are you trying to give us all a heart attack?" demanded Michael, as he pulled his sister away from the overhang.

Truthfully, his heart was pounding a mile a minute. He didn't know if he wanted to hug his sister or knock some sense into her. If it hadn't been for that cat's mewing, Bridget might have been seriously hurt.

Michael quickly guided the children down the ladder and out the door, praying to all their guardian angels as hard as he could. He said a special thank you to Bridget's angel since he figured she had worked overtime to keep the child from falling.

Once again, thinking about that close call both frightened him and made him mad. What was she thinking?

"Here, Mama Cat," called Bridget.

"That's what she was thinking," decided Michael.

He watched in surprise as Mama Cat walked up to his sibling. Since she hadn't approached any of them in the days she had been with them, he guessed the feline had finally decided they were safe to be around.

"You need to give Mama Cat a medal," declared Hunter. "She saved your life."

Mama Cat stood up straight at that compliment. She was a real, live heroine! The stories she would have to tell her babies!

CHAPTER 8
Consequences

Bridget sat on the top step of the front porch. Her hunched little figure made the two-story house look even bigger than usual. Maggy was lying beside Bridget and Mama Cat was lying on the porch swing.

As Bridget sighed deeply, they both looked at her.

"It's not fair," she said to the animals. "I knew I wasn't going to fall. I was just trying to make friends with you, Mama Cat."

Bridget could still hear her mother's words as Michael and Hunter told her about the episode in the barn.

"The barn is off limits to you, young lady. As a matter of fact, I think a day without any pool, television, or computer privileges would give you some time to think about the danger you were in!"

"But, Mommy!" Bridget had protested.

"Whining gets you nowhere except sent to your room," warned her mother.

"Okay," huffed Bridget. "I'm going to sit on the front porch. At least Maggy and Mama Cat like me."

So there she was, alone on the porch, contemplating her problems.

A day without the pool, the television, and the computer! Boy, her mother was mean. Just wait, Bridget thought. When I get to be the mother, I'm always going to let my children do whatever they want!

The screen door slammed, startling Bridget out of her thoughts.

"It's not so bad, Bridget," said Hunter, coming out to sit beside his little sister. "We all do things we shouldn't do. Remember when I accidentally let the pigs out of the pigpen? I was grounded for a week!"

Bridget giggled as she thought about that incident. Everyone in the family had chased those three pigs up and down the hills. Michael had made a running leap for one of them and landed in the mud. When he sat up, he grinned as he held a squealing, wiggling pig in his arms. "One down, two to go," he had called to them.

Mr. Brown and Hunter had collided as they jumped for the same pig. It was just like in the cartoons. Her daddy and Hunter were lying on the ground, rubbing their heads. Mommy was asking them if they were okay. And the poor little pig was running as fast as he could down the hill towards the creek!

Bridget could even remember standing at the pigpen calling for the pigs. "Here piggy, piggy," she had yelled at the fleeing swine.

"Bridget, you don't get pigs to come by calling 'here, piggy, piggy,'" Hunter had told her.

"Well, you don't get them by butting heads with Daddy, either," she had retorted.

"All right, you two, stop fussing with each other and keep chasing those pigs!" she remembered their mother had yelled over her shoulder, as she took off after the animals.

Eventually the pigs got tired of running and decided they wanted to eat. They came home and walked right into their pen! Afterwards, her mom had declared that the best thing about pigs was bacon!

"Well now," said Michael, as he rubbed his hand in Bridget's curls. "If y'all think a day and a week are bad, you should try a month!"

"Remember when Dad went out of town and I was in charge of feeding the cows? I misjudged the distance between the tractor and the truck. I stabbed the back of the truck with the hayfork. It was just like opening a can of sardines. I'll never forget that sound. And I'll never forget Dad's face when he saw his new truck. I didn't know faces could get that red except in cartoons! What's worse is that we still have the truck and

I'm reminded of my mistake every day!"

By this time, all three Brown children were laughing at their bloopers. The more they thought about them, the funnier the incidents became. Pretty soon Bridget was laughing so hard she was crying.

They were still giggling when Mr. Brown pulled into the driveway after his day at work.

"Now this is what I like to come home to—happy children. You three certainly must have had a good day," he said to them.

You'd be surprised, thought Mama Cat, as she watched the children double over at their father's remark. You'd be very surprised.

CHAPTER 9
The Milkmaid

The next day Mama Cat decided to follow Mrs. Brown around as she did her chores. She watched as Mrs. Brown hung clothes on the line in the backyard. She was amazed when Mrs. Brown started talking to her. "Well, good morning, Mama Cat. And how are you today?"

Now what am I supposed to say to that? wondered Mama Cat. Doesn't she know I don't speak her language? She decided a meow would do.

"You're looking good, not as frightened as you used to. I'm certainly glad you decided to stay with us. If you hadn't been here, who knows what would have happened to Bridget!" continued Mrs. Brown.

My goodness, thought Mama Cat. A human being is actually grateful to me. I must be worthwhile after all.

"I guess you're going to be needing a place for your kittens," said Mrs. Brown. "After I milk the goat, I'll show you the back sheds. There's hay in them and a lock on the door so large animals can't get in. Oh, but don't worry, there's a hole in the bottom of the door that should be just about your size."

Mama Cat's ears perked up at this information. She'd noticed the sheds out back, but she'd been so busy observing the Brown children and their friends that she hadn't taken the time to do more than walk by them.

"Okay, Mama Cat, let's go milk that goat," said Mrs. Brown. "I expect she's ready to see me by now."

"Good morning, Daisy," Mrs. Brown said to the white nanny goat standing down the hill on the left side of the house. The goat glanced up and gave a "maaa" in response to the greeting. She stopped chewing her kudzu and walked over to her caretaker.

Mama Cat just stared at the scene. This lady must talk to all the animals, she thought to herself.

Mrs. Brown sat beside the goat on the small three-legged stool she had brought with her. She gave Daisy some sweet feed to keep her occupied and she began talking to Daisy as she milked her.

"Do you remember the first time I tried to milk you, Daisy?" she asked the goat. "You would have gotten a good laugh at that, Mama Cat; wouldn't she, Daisy?"

"There I was, a city girl born and bred, trying to figure out how I was going to milk a goat. I'd seen goats on my grandma's farm, but I'd never seen one milked," continued Mrs. Brown. "I thought it was going to be easy. After all, the movies made it look easy to milk a cow, and a goat is smaller than a cow. Boy, was I wrong.

"First I had to overcome my embarrassment. Since I'd never milked a goat before, of course I'd never touched a goat's teats. What a time I had! I'd pull on the teat, and I could feel the milk, but it went back up into the udder instead of coming out! It was like squeezing a water balloon and feeling the water go up.

"I got so frustrated. And the poor calf I was supposed to give the milk to was standing by the fence bawling at me because he was hungry. To top it off, Jezebel and her kittens were all rubbing against my legs just like they knew fresh milk was nearby!"

Mama Cat listened to this monologue with amusement. She could just imagine the red-haired woman trying to milk a goat with mewing cats and a crying calf.

"When I finally figured out the right way to move my fingers to get the milk to come out, I shot the milk right in Jezebel's face. Poor cat. She hadn't planned on a milk attack!"

Mama Cat got tickled as the story proceeded. Suddenly it got to be too much for the feline. Strange noises started coming from her. She even lay down on the grass and started rolling from side to side!

"Why, Mama Cat," exclaimed Mrs. Brown. "I do believe you're laughing at me!"

And so she was.

CHAPTER 10
Her Favorite Room

The back sheds were wonderful!

The sheds were actually three separate rooms under one long rectangular roof. Each room was about twelve feet wide and fifteen feet long. Mama Cat wondered why she hadn't investigated these from the very beginning.

One of the shed's rooms held a corn sheller. You could put a dry ear of corn in one end of the sheller, turns its handle and watch the bare ear come out of the other end while the kernels fell from a hole at the bottom of the sheller. Against one of the walls of the room was a corn bin that held the ears of corn.

There wasn't much corn left since it was from last year's crop; but by combining the shelled corn with chicken feed, there was plenty for the chickens to eat. Several covered barrels marked sweet feed (for goats), cat food, and dog food lined another wall.

The middle shed compartment held rakes, shovels, hoes, and other pieces of equipment used around the yard area. From its ceiling hung baskets filled with dried herbs. A potting table ladened with flower gardening supplies was pushed against the far wall. Someone had even run an electric line in this shed and when they entered the room Mrs. Brown pulled a string and a ceiling fan started turning as a light came on.

"This is my favorite room, Mama Cat," said Mrs. Brown. "It has everything I need to work in my flower beds. I even pot some of our vegetables in here early in the spring. Then I bring them into the house and place them in a window with a southern exposure. When it's time to plant them outside, I've got a head start."

"The next room is the one I think you'll like for your kittens, Mama Cat," continued Mrs. Brown.

Mrs. Brown was right. Mama Cat thought the last room was perfect for her kittens.

It held nothing but bales of hay, all stacked and lined against the walls. The hay's sweet smell filled the cubicle. There was a small hole in the bottom of the door that was the perfect size for Mama Cat to walk through. Two windows covered with screen let the air flow into the room. Mama Cat's babies would be safe here.

"We can bring a water bowl and a food bowl out here for you, so you won't have to leave your little ones," Mrs. Brown explained to Mama Cat. "I know how protective we mothers can be with our babies. We don't want to let them out of our sight for a minute."

Mama Cat jumped onto a hay bale. She began looking for one that might be surrounded by several others, kind of like a fenced-in yard. After a couple of minutes, she found exactly what she wanted. Someone had taken a bale of hay from the inside row and left the others sitting around it. Perfect!

"I can see you know just what you're doing, Mama Cat," said Mrs. Brown. "I'll just close the door behind me."

Mama Cat yawned. Goodness, I'm tired. She stretched out to take a nap on the hay.

She awoke to the sound of voices in the feed shed next door.

"You try it first, Lori," urged Bridget.

"No way, you try it first," responded Lori.

"Suppose we try it together?" suggested Bridget. "Maggy likes it. And she likes our food too. So her food should taste good to us."

"Okay," agreed Lori.

Bridget and Lori plunged their hands into the barrel marked dog food. They made sure they each had one of the various shapes and colors of the food.

"Let's try the yellow, bone-shaped one first," said Lori.

"Okay, we'll try it on the count of three," said Bridget. "One, two, three!"

"Hmm. This tastes pretty good. No wonder Maggy likes it. Let's try the others," urged Bridget.

Lori nodded in agreement and the girls continued to munch away at the pieces of dog food.

"It's sweet," said Lori in a surprised voice. "I didn't know they made dog food sweet. Do you think cat food will taste this good?"

"I don't know," answered Bridget, "but there's a barrel of it right here.

Oh, dear, thought Mama Cat. What will those girls think of next?

Just then, Mama Cat heard Mrs. Brown calling for the girls.

"Coming, Mommy," yelled Bridget.

She and Lori put the top back on the dog food barrel and hurried towards the house.

"Lori's mother just called. She's on her way to pick up the girls. Let's make sure they have their bags ready to go," Mrs. Brown told Bridget and Lori.

As the girls helped Mrs. Brown gather Lori and Stacy's things, Mrs. Brown started sniffing the air.

"I declare I smell dog food. I wonder if Maggy has hidden some food somewhere in the living room," she said. "You know how she likes to have some food for later. You'd think we never fed her."

Bridget and Lori just looked at each other.

"Um, Mommy," stammered Bridget. "I don't think Maggy hid her food in here."

"You know how good Maggy's food always looks? Well, we decided we wanted to see if it tasted as good as it looked. So we ate some," Bridget quickly continued. She was going to get the words out fast, before she lost her nerve.

"You did what?" asked her mother in a pretty loud voice.

"We ate some dog food," replied Bridget in a much quieter voice.

"Bridget Noelle and Lori Diana! Dog food is for dogs. It is not for people. Remember how we've talked about not eating things that are not for us?" asked Mrs. Brown.

"Dog food is definitely one of the foods we do not eat. The next time you two decide you want to try something new to eat, ask me about it first. We'll decide together if it's something you can have," suggested Mrs. Brown.

"Yes, ma'am," Bridget and Lori responded.

"Mommy?" Bridget asked, as Mrs. Brown pulled a stray sandal of Lori's from under the sofa.

"Yes, honey," came her mother's muffled reply.

"Did you know that dog food was sweet?"

Mrs. Brown's shoulders started shaking with laughter.

"I believe that's the same thing your brothers told me when they decided to taste the dog food," she told her astonished daughter, as she walked out of the room.

CHAPTER 11
Storm Watch

"Whoa, Michael, look at those clouds," exclaimed Hunter.

Hunter and Michael had just ridden their bikes up the gravel driveway into the front yard. They were returning from a bike ride into town. Taking off their helmets, they walked the bicycles to the tool shop off the side of the house. Experience had taught them to put their bikes away as soon as they got off them.

"They sure are black," responded Michael. "And angry looking. You can even see the lightning in the distance. I guess we'd better see if Mom has already drawn water in case we lose electricity."

Mama Cat was eyeing the same dark clouds from beside the back sheds.

Well, she thought, I guess I'll find out if there are any leaks in the shed roof. Better to know now than when I have my kittens.

She made her way back into her new home to wait out the approaching storm.

In the house, Mrs. Brown was looking worriedly out the back kitchen window.

"Those clouds are certainly coming fast. Whoever lives where they are now is probably having a terrible storm," she told the children.

"I've already taken the clothes off the line and drawn water. Michael, would you get out the flashlights, candles, and matches and put them on the kitchen table, please?" she requested of her oldest child.

Without waiting for his reply, she turned to her next oldest son. "Hunter, you and your dad did check the generator last week, right?"

"Yes, ma'am. It was fine. Dad set it up so that we can use it with no problems," he answered.

"Good. And Bridget, you make sure Maggy and Miss Kitty have food and water. If we lose power, we

want to make sure they're taken care of," Mrs. Brown explained to her youngest.

"What about Mama Cat?" questioned Bridget.

"I fed and watered her about an hour ago. She'll be fine in the hay shed out back."

"Do you think Lori and Stacy are home yet?" Bridget scrunched her face up in worry as she posed this question.

"I'm sure they are, honey. They left about thirty minutes ago and it only takes them twenty minutes to get from our house to theirs. You can give them a quick call if you want," Mrs. Brown told her daughter.

As Bridget called her friends, Mrs. Brown thought about life in the country.

When a storm approached here, you had to make sure you had supplies on hand to survive without electricity. Even though it did not happen often, when the power was knocked out by a storm, it could be hours or days before it was restored. The power company did its best to get the electricity back on, but sometimes it took a lot of manpower and many hours to correct the problem. It was always better to be prepared than to be caught unawares.

Michael and Hunter commented to their mother that the cows were lying down in the pasture, a sure sign of a change in the weather. The chickens, goats, and pigs were in their respective houses.

The wind began to pick up. Trees started blowing so hard their leaves dropped to the ground. The sky turned black as night.

A screeching noise and a crashing sound came from the roof. The side door was ripped off its hinges.

"Mommy," asked Bridget in fright, "what is happening? We don't have storms like this."

"I don't know, honey, but let's stay away from the windows until this tempest is over," suggested Mrs. Brown.

As the family sat in the middle of the house, they listened to hail as it pounded the tin roof. Then came torrents of rain. It sounded like the heavens had opened up and let everything fall to the earth.

The next sound they heard was "crack, crack, crack." It sounded like trees were falling over. One minute the group was sitting in a well-lit dining room, and the next minute it was sitting in darkness. The trees had obviously taken a power line down with them.

"Holy cow, this must be the storm of the century," exclaimed Michael.

"I wonder if it's a hurricane or a tornado?" asked Hunter.

"I don't care what you call it," said Bridget, "I just want it to be over."

As if it heard her, the wind stopped roaring. Then the rain halted.

Everything was so quiet; it was spooky.

"Can we look outside now, Mom?" Hunter wanted to know.

"Let's watch from the front porch first; if things look okay from there, we'll check on the animals," stated his mother.

The family was totally unprepared for the sight before it.

Trees had been uprooted, both on the hillside and across the road. Lawn furniture was sitting in trees. As they walked around the house, Michael pointed out the large sycamore tree branch that had fallen on the backside of the building.

"How is Daddy going to get home, Mommy?" worried Bridget.

"I'm not sure, Bridget, but I know he'll find a way. We'll call him on the cell phone right now."

Several minutes later, after reassuring his family that he was indeed okay, Mr. Brown ended the phone call with the words that he would be home when he could get there. As trees were down all over, it might be some time.

Comforted by the fact that their father was fine, the children and Mrs. Brown checked on the farm animals.

By this time, the animals were out of their houses, pecking the ground and munching on the wet grass as though nothing had happened.

"Oh, look, Mama Cat has come to see us," shouted Bridget in delight. "I was afraid she might have her babies during that storm," she added.

"I know that storm seemed forever to you, honey, but it really only lasted fifteen minutes. It takes longer than that for kittens to be born," explained Mrs. Brown.

"Well, on TV, babies are always born during storms," declared the child.

"Bridget," said Hunter, "that's television; this is real life."

"Look at it this way, Bridget," commented Michael, "this will give Mama Cat more time to really trust you so that when she does have her kittens, she'll let you pet them."

As she listened to the siblings discuss her, Mama Cat smiled to herself. She already had decided that she trusted the entire Brown family. After all, they had given her a nice dry home and food and water. Best of all, they treated her with kindness. What more could she want?

CHAPTER 12
The New Arrivals

Mama Cat had the answer to that question the very next day.

She wanted someone to stay with her while she was having her kittens. Mama Cat had never had kittens before and although she thought she would be fine, she still wanted company.

Mr. Brown had arrived home several hours after yesterday evening's storm. He told the family the reason he made it home that soon was because people in the country had power saws and weren't afraid to use them. Rather than wait for utility company personnel to reach them, people had simply taken their saws, cut up the fallen trees blocking the road and removed the obstacles. Because of this initiative, the county roads were passable by midnight so that those who worked in the city could get home.

It also helped speed up the process of restoring electricity. Some homes had regained electricity by early morning; however, others were still using flashlights, candles, and generators.

The Brown family spent the day after "the storm of the century," as Michael had dubbed it, cleaning up debris around the house. They were grateful to have a chlorinated swimming pool because after all the hauling of dead branches and checking on fence lines in the pasture, they were a hot, sweaty bunch. The pool was the perfect solution.

"I sure am glad Uncle Steven gave us the pool kit to build this pool," commented Hunter, as he floated in the clear, cool water.

"Me, too," replied Michael, "although the installation was not one of my favorite activities."

"Well, Daddy liked using the backhoe to dig the hole for the pool," piped in Bridget, as she played on the steps in the shallow end of the rectangular pool.

"That's because that was the fun part," answered Michael. "Being down in that hole, digging the sides to make them even was hot, dirty work. And trying to get the vermiculite mixture just right was awful. But I did learn that I didn't want to put in pools for a living. That experience made me realize that college could be a terrific idea."

"I'm glad to hear that," remarked his mother. "I'm sure Uncle Steven will also be glad to hear that he has helped to encourage you to go to college."

"Just remember how good college looks when you have a lot of homework or a hard test to study for," reminded his dad.

"Don't remind me of tests, Dad," said Michael. "It's summer, I want to enjoy it."

Mama Cat, who had been sitting beneath the sycamore tree near the pool, decided it was time to interrupt the family so that she could make her wishes known.

"Meow, meow, meow."

"I wonder what's wrong with Mama Cat," said Bridget, as she climbed out of the pool to check on the animal.

As Bridget approached Mama Cat, the feline turned around and started walking to her home in the back shed.

"If something's wrong, Mama Cat, why are you walking away from me?" the little girl asked.

"Meow, meow, meow."

"Mommy, what's wrong with Mama Cat?"

"I don't know, honey, but give me a minute to dry off and I'll go with you to see what we can find out," answered her mother.

Mother and daughter held hands as they walked to the back shed. When they opened the door, they looked around for Mama Cat.

"Here she is, Bridget, between these hay bales," Mrs. Brown called to her child. "It looks like she's trying to get comfortable to have her kittens. How odd, though. Most cats like their privacy."

"Wow," said Bridget. "Can I go get Daddy and the boys?"

"Let's wait a while and see what happens before we have the whole family in here," answered her mother.

A short while later, Bridget and Mrs. Brown watched as Mama Cat gave birth to her first kitten. They watched as she licked the birth sack off the baby and cleaned her up.

Bridget's eyes were as big as saucers. "Look at her, Mommy. This is so cool. Now can I get the boys?"

No sooner had Bridget posed this question than the rest of the family showed up at the shed door. Mama Cat looked up as she heard them enter the room.

"Hush, y'all," cautioned Mrs. Brown. "Mama Cat is having her kittens. It appears she wants company, but not noisy company."

The entire family watched as Mama Cat gave birth to two more kittens.

"She's so quiet about it," commented Hunter, as he gazed at the new mother and her babies. "And she looks like she's concentrating really hard."

"It's amazing, isn't it?" asked Michael.

"I certainly have a lot of admiration for Mama Cat," said Mrs. Brown. "I was never that quiet when I had you three."

"Amen to that," affirmed her husband, as he nodded his head.

Mama Cat chose this particular moment to deliver one more kitten. She cleaned this one and gathered all her young close. The babes immediately began mewing as they tried to nurse for the first time. She looked upon her young ones with pride. One was gray with white stripes, one was dark orange striped, one was light orange striped, and one was black with a splash of white on its face and paws. What a gorgeous litter she had!

"What a wonderful end to this day," said Mrs. Brown. "Thank you, Mama Cat. You've given us a beautiful gift."

"Does this mean that Mama Cat can stay forever?" asked Bridget.

"Yes, Bridget, Mama Cat can stay forever," answered her father.

Mama Cat sighed with pure pleasure. This was a wonderful end to the day.

Author's Note

Writing a book is not just about telling a story; it's about sharing a piece of yourself with others and hoping they will be receptive. This book came about because many years ago, my husband asked me what I wanted to do when I grew up. I told him I wanted to write books. It only took thirty years, honey. Thanks for asking me.

Mama Cat's story was inspired by my family, by Mama Cat and by the grace of God. Thanks to my wonderful children who served as the characters in this book—the real Michael, Hunter and Bridget. I'm so glad I shared in your childhood. And, yes, I know I changed the facts. Thanks also to their cousins and friends, who had no idea when they came to play that they might find themselves in a book one day.

I'd also like to thank my parents, Aunt Birdie, my siblings and daughter-in-law for their support. It's comforting to know you are always there.

Thanks to my former students at Appomattox County High School and to my colleagues in Family, Career and Community Leaders of America. You expanded my definition of family.

Thanks to my current colleagues at the Alliance for Families and Children of Central Virginia. Your support is just like that quilt.

Thanks to Debbie Hamlett, librarian extraordinaire, who was the first "outsider" to read my book. Your encouragement and reading of the book to countless second graders gave me the courage to continue.

Thanks to Gail Gray for showing me the way.

Thanks to Debra Jones for over two decades of listening.

Thanks to Joyce Maddox for your expertise as my editor.

And finally, thanks be to God!!

About the Author

Marcie Jones is a former early childhood education teacher. During her fourteen years in the classroom, she was honored several times in *Who's Who Among America's Teachers*. She was named Appomattox Teacher of the Year and was a nominee for the Disney Teacher of the Year Award. Mrs. Jones is currently working on her second "Mama Cat" book. She lives with her husband in Spout Spring, Virginia.

About the Illustrator

Henry "Hank" J. Kouche, is an award-winning designer, art director and illustrator. He lives and works in the Lake Lanier area of North Georgia with his sweetheart Janis and three cats: Patchouli, Jolene, and Clarence. Hank is a veteran visual communicator, presently pursuing new areas of personal creative expression in many forms, metaphors and mediums.